The Yellow House

Vincent van Gogh & Paul Gauguin Side by Side

By Susan Goldman Rubin · Illustrations by Jos. A. Smith

Published in association with The Art Institute of Chicago
Harry N. Abrams, Inc., Publishers

One day in the spring of 1888 Vincent van Gogh put on his straw hat, gathered his art supplies, and went out to paint. Peach trees, irises, and buttercups bloomed in the orchards and meadows. But Vincent's favorite was the sunflowers.

At the end of the day, when Vincent finished painting, he returned to his Yellow House. Because he had just recently moved to Arles, a town in the south of France, he had only a few friends—the postman and his family, a soldier, and Monsieur and Madame Ginoux, who owned the café down the street where Vincent often ate dinner. "Days go by without my speaking a word to anyone," Vincent wrote to his brother Theo, who was an art dealer in Paris.

Like many artists, Vincent worked long hours by himself. But he missed the company of other people, especially artists who could discuss painting. He hoped that warm, sunny Arles would attract fellow painters to join him. Together they would form a kind of family of artists, a Studio of the South.

In Paris the year before, Vincent had met many painters. The ones he most admired were the Impressionists. Fascinated with how natural light, times of day, and weather affect the way things look, they inspired him to change the colors of his paintings from browns, blacks, and grays to much brighter shades of blue, pink, and green. The Impressionists also helped him learn to paint exactly what he saw with his own eyes—boats on the river, the countryside, flowers, and people.

But another artist, Paul Gauguin, particularly impressed Vincent because he was doing something entirely different. Paul painted pictures from his imagination—feelings, fantasies, and dreams. Paul was far away in Brittany, in the northern part of France. "Perhaps Gauguin will come south," Vincent wrote his brother. Theo thought this was a good idea. The two artists could spend a year together in Arles and work side by side. Theo sent Paul a letter inviting him to join Vincent in the Yellow House. Paul accepted the invitation.

When Vincent learned that Paul had agreed to come, he was so excited that he began to get everything ready in the Yellow House. He installed gas lamps so that they could paint inside at night, and he bought a bed for the guest room. "Now that I hope to live with Gauguin in a studio of our own," Vincent wrote to Theo, "I want to make decorations. . . . Nothing but big flowers." So Vincent made bright new pictures of sunflowers to hang in the guest room. He also painted pictures of the little park across the street and hung those up, too.

On October 23, 1888, Paul arrived in Arles. Vincent was delighted! The weather was perfect, so the two artists set out to paint right away.

Like Vincent, Paul quickly realized that the sun was hotter and brighter in the south than it was in Paris or Brittany. The colors of the sky, the buildings, and the flowers glowed vividly. Even the people looked different! Thrilled at what they saw, Vincent and Paul felt inspired to paint.

But each man went about it in his own way. Although Vincent and Paul shared their art supplies—charcoal, paints, and canvases—they used them differently. Vincent liked to load his brush with lots of paint and put it on the canvas in dots and dashes.

"My brush stroke has no system at all," he once wrote to an artist friend. "I hit the canvas with irregular touches of the brush, which I leave as they are." Thick swirls of strong colors expressed his feelings—his love of nature, his joy in painting.

Paul painted more slowly than Vincent. He loved nature, too, but he would wait and dream about what he saw before he started to make a picture. He did not squeeze paint straight out of the tubes onto the canvas like Vincent sometimes did. Instead Paul blended the paints on his palette, making new colors that matched his dreams. He spread the paints smoothly in careful shapes.

At night the two artists talked about painting. For instance, they each had favorite colors. Paul could tell what color Vincent liked from the way he had decorated the house: "In my yellow room, sunflowers with purple eyes stood out against a yellow background. The yellow sun shone through the yellow curtains. Oh yes, the good Vincent loved yellow." Paul, however, really adored red.

Each used his favorite color in portraits of Madame Ginoux, the wife of the café owner. The artists asked her to come to the Yellow House to pose.

Vincent's portrait has a bright yellow background. As usual, he painted quickly and made his picture in less than an hour. He was probably finished by the time Madame Ginoux had to go back to work. Paul only had time to make a drawing. Later he went to the café to do more drawings. Then he returned to the house and put his drawings together to compose a scene showing not only Madame Ginoux, but also her customers, a pool table, and even a little cat. The background in this painting is bright red. Vincent showed Madame Ginoux in the daytime, dressed and ready to go out. Her parasol (to protect her from the hot sun) and gloves lie on the table. Paul, however, created a nighttime scene of the smoky café. Madame smiles a little as she glances at the sleepy group behind her.

Vincent and Paul spent many evenings discussing the best way to paint. Often their discussions developed into quarrels. But they did agree that they could learn from each other. Paul told Vincent to try painting something he saw only in his imagination, not in real life. Vincent imagined his mother and sister in a garden back home in Holland. He picked colors that he thought expressed their personalities, and used small dots of paint. The painting was an experiment for him. He worked on it at home when the cold November weather made painting outdoors unpleasant.

Usually Vincent aimed to complete a painting in one sitting—by the time the sun set or a rain shower forced him to stop for the day. But now, working inside on this painting, he could not be sure when it was finished. He worked on it so long that he thought he had spoiled it. "I think that you also need practice for work from the imagination," Vincent wrote to Theo. He did not like this imaginary garden as much as the real garden in front of the Yellow House.

Paul then painted a garden. Maybe he felt it was easier to teach
Vincent by showing him rather than telling him how he worked. In
Paul's painting there are four women coming down a curved path
alongside grass and plants. The picture has a mysterious mood. A
red fence blocks the way. A large green bush seems to have a face.

Living and working together turned out to be difficult for the two artists. They clashed in many ways. Vincent was messy and careless. Paul was neat and organized. Vincent talked all the time, while Paul stayed quiet.

Vincent tried to please his roommate, but often his attempts backfired. Paul usually did the cooking, but once in a while Vincent tried to make a meal such as soup. "I have no idea what mixtures he used—they seemed like those of the colors on his canvases—but we could never eat it," Paul remembered.

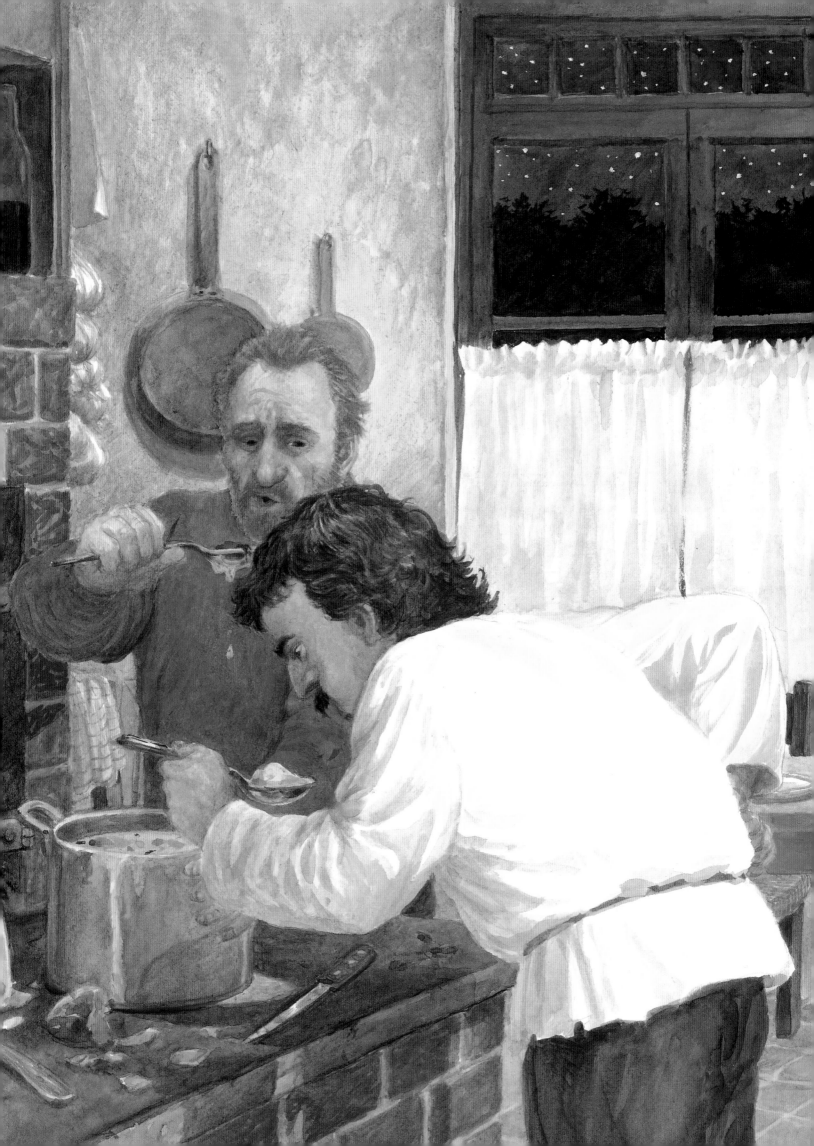

In two pictures of their chairs, Vincent expressed their differences. Vincent's chair sits on a tile floor in front of a box of onions. His chair is made of plain yellow wood, and his pipe and tobacco rest on the seat. Paul's armchair is fancier, with a curved back and a green fabric seat. It holds two books and a candle. Vincent saw himself as a simple man with simple tastes. But he viewed Paul as a thinker who liked nice things.

While Paul sometimes found Vincent irritating, he appreciated how hard Vincent worked and how much he loved nature. He expressed his admiration in a portrait he made of Vincent painting sunflowers, which he gave to Theo as a gift.

By December, however, Paul wrote to Theo that he wanted to return to Paris. Vincent guessed how he felt, and it greatly upset him. The last two weeks of the year were cold and terribly windy. The two artists were cooped up in the Yellow House. One night they got into a fight. Vincent became very angry and almost attacked Paul. Instead he hurt himself by cutting off part of his own ear. Vincent was taken to the hospital, and a frightened Paul quickly left Arles.

Although they never met face to face again, Vincent and Paul exchanged letters. They still admired each other's art, and they got along much better as pen pals than as roommates! Vincent told Paul to keep the sunflower paintings he had made for him. Paul gave Vincent his drawing of Madame Ginoux, and later Vincent did a painting based on it. When Paul saw the painting, he wrote to Vincent, "I like it better than my drawing."

Through their letters, Vincent and Paul continued to encourage each other. The pictures they made during the two months they lived together in the Yellow House are some of the most important and beautiful of their careers. Working side by side, the artists inspired and challenged each other. Today the paintings still glow with their emotion and energy.

VINCENT VAN GOGH

Vincent van Gogh was born on March 30, 1853, in Zundert, a village in Holland. He was the oldest of six children. As a boy Vincent began to show signs of suffering from strange, depressed moods. Throughout his life he found it hard to get along with people, although he desperately craved company. His few romances ended unhappily, and he never married.

As a child Vincent drew quite well, but he did not decide to become an artist until he was 27 years old. First Vincent held five other jobs—art gallery assistant, teacher, preacher, social worker helping poor coal miners, and clerk. When he finally applied to art school he was turned down because the teachers did not think he had much talent. So Vincent taught himself how to draw and paint.

In 1885 Vincent completed an early masterpiece, *Potato Eaters*, painted in dark colors to suggest the hardships of peasant life. When he went to Paris the following year and saw Impressionist paintings, he changed his own palette to lighter, brighter colors. Vincent also discovered Japanese prints, which greatly influenced his work. He loved painting so much that he used up his money on art supplies instead of food. Working long hours without eating made Vincent sick. In 1888 he moved to Arles, in the south of France, hoping that the warm sun would make him better.

Vincent rented the Yellow House and believed it would become a gathering place for other artists, the Studio of the South. He was thrilled when Paul Gauguin came to stay with him. Even though he and Paul learned much from each other, they clashed, and their arguments contributed to Vincent having a breakdown. In a fit of madness on December 23, 1888, he had the urge to hurt himself, and he cut off part of his ear. The next day he went to a hospital, then briefly returned to the Yellow House. But people in town thought he was crazy.

They signed a petition demanding that he be locked up in a mental hospital. Vincent himself decided to enter a mental asylum in Saint Rémy in spring of 1889. By 1890 he had recovered and moved to Auvers-sur-Oise, a village near Paris. There he painted the wheat fields and farmers. But he suffered another fit on July 27, 1890, and shot himself. Two days later, at the age of 37, he died. His brother Theo died a few months later, and Theo's wife devoted herself to gaining recognition for Vincent's work. But not until the 1920s did the world begin to appreciate the art of Vincent van Gogh.

During his lifetime Vincent sold only one painting, which he completed in Arles. Today his paintings and drawings are loved by millions of people. Most of these masterpieces belong to the world's greatest museums, where crowds wait on line to see them. Once Vincent wrote to Theo, "I cannot help it that my pictures do not sell. Nevertheless the time will come when people will see that they are worth more than the price of the paint."

PAUL GAUGUIN

Paul Gauguin, like Vincent van Gogh, did not decide to become an artist until he was an adult—35 years old. And like Vincent, he, too, was mostly self-taught.

Paul was born in France in 1848. When he was eighteen months old he moved to Lima, Peru, with his parents and sister. On the way Paul's father died, and Paul and his family stayed with his mother's relatives. They returned to France when Paul was six, but he loved Lima and never forgot it. Throughout his life he searched for other colorful, exotic places.

Back in France Paul went to school. Then at age 17 he joined the merchant navy. On a year-long trip around the world he had his first glimpse of Tahiti, a French colony. The tropical island seemed like paradise to him, and he dreamed of returning someday.

When Paul was twenty he settled down in Paris and became a stockbroker. In 1873 he met and married a young Danish woman, Mette Sophie Gad. Over the next ten years they had five children—four boys and a girl. During that period Paul started painting as a hobby and also studied sculpting and ceramics. Just at that time the Impressionists began exhibiting their work. Paul became friends with them, and soon they invited Paul to exhibit his work with theirs. In 1883 he decided to give up his job and become a full-time artist.

Now Paul had no means of supporting his family. His wife moved back to Denmark with the children. He missed them terribly, but he was determined to fulfill his goal. He wrote to a friend, "I can only do one thing: Paint." He moved to Brittany, a picturesque area in France that appealed to him because it looked primitive.

On a trip to Paris in 1886 he met Vincent van Gogh and his brother Theo. Paul still dreamed of finding his tropical paradise and scraped together enough money to sail to Panama, and from there to the French colony of Martinique. When he came down with dysentery, he had to return to France for medical care. At this point Vincent and Theo invited him to come to the Yellow House. Paul accepted their offer mainly because he was sick and broke, yet wanted to keep painting.

From the start Paul realized he had made a mistake. He and Vincent were so different that they could not live together easily. But the eight weeks he spent with Vincent powerfully influenced his work. Later he even wound up painting sunflowers, Vincent's favorite subject.

After Vincent's death in 1890, Paul made two trips to Tahiti and produced his most unique art. Inspired by the lush scenery and beautiful natives, he did dozens of paintings and made hundreds of sketches he later developed into finished works. Back in Paris after the first trip, Paul exhibited his paintings. Although critics and young artists praised his originality, only eleven paintings were sold. People were shocked by the bright, glowing colors and strange figures and scenes. Even the titles sounded odd: *Are You Jealous?* and *We Shall Not Go to Market Today*. Paul stayed in Paris for a while and wrote about Tahiti, explaining the symbols in his paintings.

On his second trip to Tahiti he produced some of his finest work. This time when he sent paintings back to Paris they sold. Meanwhile, Paul's health grew worse. He suffered from a series of heart attacks, and a serious skin rash that would not heal, and then an eye infection that prevented him from painting. In his last years he wrote a journal called *Before and After* in which he reviewed his life, including the time spent with Vincent van Gogh in Arles. Paul died in Hiva Oa, an island near Tahiti, in 1903 at the age of 54. The news did not reach Paris until two months later. Soon after, an exhibition of Paul's work attracted crowds of viewers. He once wrote, "I do not copy nature. For me everything happens in my exuberant imagination."

Author's Note

As a children's book writer, my goal has been to introduce young people to the pleasure of looking at art. So I was thrilled to be asked to write a book for children about Vincent van Gogh and Paul Gauguin working together. My research began with a trip to Chicago to meet with the curators of the upcoming exhibition "Van Gogh and Gauguin: The Studio of the South" at The Art Institute of Chicago. The curators even took me behind the scenes through a "secret door" in one of the galleries and showed me their detailed plans for the exhibit.

I flew home with a briefcase stuffed with material—letters from the artists, excerpts from journals, and chapters from critical works written by scholars. I carried a bag full of books and sent for more. Then, during eight intense weeks—the length of time that Vincent and Paul lived together in the Yellow House in Arles—I developed the manuscript. It was fascinating to find out details about their experience as roommates and the stories behind some of the paintings and drawings they made and that I knew so well.

Now I hope that young readers will find the story of the Yellow House just as interesting as I did, and enjoy the incredible art produced there by Vincent van Gogh and Paul Gauguin.

Susan Goldman Rubin

Artist's Note

This book presented an unexpected and interesting challenge. Vincent van Gogh and Paul Gauguin are among the most widely known and popular artists of the past. We feel we know them better than many other artists of their time. Both painters left self-portraits, which have established our sense of who they were and what they looked like. Suggesting the character of Gauguin was relatively simple: the likenesses we have of him include accurate self-portraits and a notable caricature, as well as posed photographs.

While van Gogh painted himself many times, he did so symbolically, changing the shape of his head, and even his eyes, in order to capture specific emotions. For instance, he wrote to his brother Theo that in one portrait he made his head rounder and his eyes more angled to look like a Japanese monk. Also, van Gogh did not like to be photographed. Today all we have is a group of beautiful interpretive paintings and Kirk Douglas's portrayal of the artist in the film *Lust for Life*. I created a van Gogh that is my best guess as to what he looked like. I viewed his paintings in a mirror (to correct the reversed likeness he painted when he looked at himself in a reflection). To this I added a sense of the artist's own written descriptions of his physical condition at the time and then used my imagination.

For the interior and exterior scenes, I am happy to report that an array of sources, from period photographs and paintings to actual objects found in museum collections, were available to help me re-create easels, brushes, lamps, chairs, beds, dinnerware, and even haystacks.

Jos. A. Smith

Selected Bibliography

Bailey, Martin, ed. *Van Gogh: Letters from Provence*. New York: Clarkson Potter, 1990.

Bernard, Bruce. *Vincent by Himself*. Boston: Little, Brown, 1985.

Brettell, Richard, Francoise Cachin, Claire Freches-Thory, Charles F. Stuckey. *The Art of Paul Gauguin*. Washington: National Gallery of Art. Chicago: The Art Institute of Chicago, 1988.

Gauguin, Paul. *Gauguin's Intimate Journals*. Mineola, New York: Dover, 1997.

Greenfield, Howard. *Paul Gauguin*. New York: Harry N. Abrams, 1993.

Hulsker, Jan. *The New Complete van Gogh*. Amsterdam: J. M. Meulenhoff. Philadelphia: John Benjamins, 1977.

Meier-Graefe, Julius. *Vincent van Gogh: A Biography*. New York: Dover, 1987.

The Museum of Modern Art, New York. *Vincent van Gogh*. Westport, Connecticut: Greenwood Press, 1935.

Nemeczek, Alfred. *Van Gogh in Arles*. Munich, London, and New York: Prestel, 1999.

Pickvance, Ronald. *Van Gogh in Arles*. New York: Harry N. Abrams, 1984.

Thomson, Belinda. *Gauguin*. London: Thames and Hudson, 1987.

———. *Gauguin by Himself*. Boston: Little, Brown, 1993.

Walther, Ingo F., and Rainer Metzger. *Vincent van Gogh: The Complete Paintings*. Cologne: Taschen, 1997.

Art Credits

Page 6 Vincent van Gogh (Dutch, 1853-1890). *Fishing in Spring*, n.d. Oil on canvas; 50.5 x 60 cm. Gift of Charles Deering McCormick, Brooks McCormick and Roger McCormick, 1965.1169. © 1994, The Art Institute of Chicago, all rights reserved.

Page 7 Paul Gauguin (French, 1848-1903). *The Vision After the Sermon: Jacob Wrestling with the Angel*, 1888. Oil on canvas; 73 x 92 cm. The National Gallery of Scotland, Edinburgh.

Page 12 Vincent van Gogh. *Madame Ginoux (L'Arlésienne)*, 1888. Oil on canvas; 92.5 x 73.5 cm. Musée d'Orsay, Paris, France. Photograph by Erich Lessing / Art Resource, NY.

Page 13 Paul Gauguin. *Night Café*, 1888. Oil on canvas, 72 x 92 cm. Pushkin Museum, Moscow.

Page 16 Vincent van Gogh. *Memory of the Garden at Etten (Ladies of Arles)*, 1888. Oil on canvas; 73.5 x 92.5 cm. The State Hermitage Museum, St. Petersburg.

Page 17 Paul Gauguin. *Old Women at Arles*, 1888. Oil on canvas; 73 x 92 cm. Mr. and Mrs. Lewis Larned Coburn Memorial Collection, 1934.391. © 1988 The Art Institute of Chicago, all rights reserved.

Plate 20, top. Vincent van Gogh. *Gauguin's Armchair*, 1888. Oil on canvas; 90.5 x 72.5 cm. Amsterdam, Van Gogh Museum (Vincent van Gogh Foundation).

Page 20, bottom. Paul Gauguin. *Portrait of Van Gogh Painting Sunflowers*, 1888. Oil on canvas; 73 x 91 cm. Amsterdam, Van Gogh Museum (Vincent van Gogh Foundation).

Page 21 Vincent van Gogh. *Van Gogh's Chair*, 1888. Oil on canvas; 91.8 x 73 cm. © National Gallery, London.

Page 28 Vincent van Gogh. *Self-portrait Dedicated to Paul Gauguin*, 1888. Oil on canvas; 59.55 x 48.26 cm. Fogg Art Museum, Harvard University, Cambridge, Massachusetts.

Page 29 Paul Gauguin. *Self-portrait with Portrait of Bernard, Les Misérables*, 1888. Oil on canvas; 45 x 55 cm. Amsterdam, Van Gogh Museum (Vincent van Gogh Foundation).

Title page, back jacket Vincent van Gogh. *Vincent's House in Arles, the "Yellow House,"* 1888. Oil on canvas; 72 x 91.5 cm. Amsterdam, Van Gogh Museum (Vincent van Gogh Foundation).

To my brother, Edwin P. Moldof—S.G.R.

To Charissa, Kari, Joe, Emily, and Andrea—J.A.S.

AUTHOR'S ACKNOWLEDGMENTS

I want to thank the following people at The Art Institute of Chicago who helped me research and write this book: Susan Rossen; Amanda Freymann; Douglas Druick; Mary Weaver; and especially Britt Salvesen for her enthusiasm and support. I also want to express my deep appreciation to Howard Reeves and Lia Ronnen at Harry N. Abrams, Inc. Special thanks to author Ann Whitford Paul. And my gratitude to George M. Nicholson for his ongoing encouragement.

ARTIST'S ACKNOWLEDGMENTS

I want to thank Valerie Demianchuk, a very talented artist and friend, who gave up hours of her precious studio time, unasked, to do picture research I would have done on my own. Valerie made it possible for me to meet a short deadline. I also thank Howard Reeves for his trust.

The illustrations were done in watercolor and gouache on paper.

Designer: Edward Miller

Library of Congress Cataloging-in-Publication Data

Rubin, Susan Goldman.
    The yellow house : Vincent van Gogh and Paul Gauguin side by side / by Susan Goldman Rubin ; illustrated by Jos. A. Smith.
        p. cm.
    "Published in association with the Art Institute of Chicago."
    ISBN 0-8109-4588-6
    1. Gogh, Vincent van, 1853-1890—Juvenile literature. 2. Gauguin,
    Paul, 1848-1903—Juvenile literature. 3. Painters—France—Biography—Juvenile literature.
    [1. Gogh, Vincent van, 1853-1890. 2. Gauguin, Paul, 1848-1903. 3. Artists.]
    I. Smith, Joseph A. (Joseph Anthony) [date], ill. II. Title.
ND653.G7 R74 2001
759.4'918—dc21   2001000455

Published in 2001 by Harry N. Abrams, Incorporated, New York
Printed and bound in Hong Kong
10 9 8 7 6 5 4 3 2

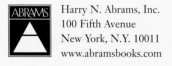

Harry N. Abrams, Inc.
100 Fifth Avenue
New York, N.Y. 10011
www.abramsbooks.com

4/0